TAKEN BY HER STEPFATHER

AGE GAP YOUNG ADULT DADDY ROMANCE

DADDY'S NAUGHTY GIRLS
BOOK FOUR

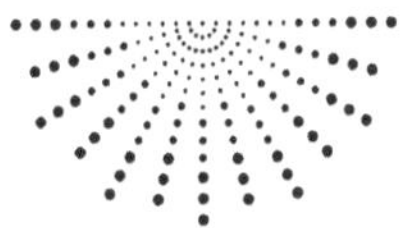

LEE RILEY

* * *

DO YOU LIKE SEXY TABOO AGE-GAP STORIES? Then this collection of erotic stories is just the right thing for you. Because these daddies know exactly what lesson to teach to these young women. And it's going to be hard, fast and unprotected...

Erotic short stories that offer hot action with stepfathers, inexperienced virgins, first times, explicit hardcore scenes and lots of cherry popping. This anthology is your chance to indulge your kinky sexual fantasies. Dive into a world of exciting and hot sex adventures. You won't regret it.

The following stories are included:

Daddy's Good Girl

Carissa faces a daunting crossroads after being expelled from college. Seeking a place to live, she turns to her attractive stepdad, Brian, and his cabin in the heart of the rugged mountains. She relies on her stepfather to look out for her, and he is more than willing to fulfill that role, provided she adheres to the guidelines he sets. And so Carissa is going to be Daddy's Good Girl and take care of all his needs as well… A Mountain Man, Daddy, Praise Kink Erotica.

Daddy's Forbidden Gadget

When 18-year-old Madison takes her stepdad's forbidden Mustang for a late-night joyride with friends, she unknowingly sets off a chain of events. Stopped by the police, she learns her stepdad reported the car stolen. As the truth emerges, Madison faces consequences, and her stepfather decides to teach her a serious lesson - hard, fast and unprotected.

Taking Care of Daddy

After her mom finds a new boyfriend and asks her to leave, Jessa seeks refuge with her former stepdad, Jon. Jon warmly welcomes her into his home, and as Jessa works to get her life back on track, Jon suggests a plan to support each other. He is going to pay for school and in exchange he gets to use her body. As Jessa realizes, that she has some very forbidden thoughts about her stepdad, she is more than willing to fulfill her part of the deal…

TAKE NOTE: This short read contain descriptions of hot, graphic, sexual situations and is intended for mature 18+

Be the first to find out about all of Lee Riley's new releases, book sales, and freebies by joining her VIP Mailing List. Join today and get a FREE book -- instantly!

Check Lee Riley's website spicybestsellers.com for more books.

DADDY'S GOOD GIRL

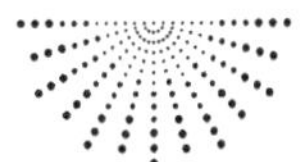

* * *

"You've got to be kidding me."

Carissa dropped the Chanel suitcase that she hadn't even begun to pay off on the worn welcome mat of her stepfather Brian's mountain cabin and took in her new surroundings.

A massive log structure, the cabin sat on a small rise at the edge of a clearing. The forest grew up thickly to its walls on three sides, only leaving a view of the narrow dirt road out the front. In the distance, a river burbled quietly through the trees.

A long flight of steps led up to a large wraparound porch, and Carissa had a brief, hopeful thought that maybe this living situation wouldn't be so bad. The porch looked promising; she could see herself sipping mimosas while snapping selfies on a Sunday morning. The light was good, and she'd been trying to post more nature content.

"You waiting for the butler?" a gruff voice said behind her before Carissa felt a smack on the ass that was too rough to be fun.

"Hey!" she protested, stumbling over her own bag. "What the hell was that--"

Before she could finish, the bag was snatched up from the ground.

"Well, come on, then," the voice said again. It was coming from a man who could only be Brian. He was dressed in a snug plaid shirt that stretched across his broad shoulders and a pair of stained jeans that he'd probably owned as long as Carissa had been alive.

Carissa couldn't help but to take a sneak peek at Brian, the man who had raised her after her mother had passed away when she was just a girl. Brian was a total asshole, of course, there was no denying that. He was obsessed with things like work and chores and not breaking the law, but Carissa couldn't help but be a little impressed with how well he was aging.

For a man who was pushing fifty, he was still pretty fit. His hair was going silver and there were crow's feet at the corners of his eyes, but Brian was still handsome in that rough, masculine way. Carissa had never given much thought to her stepfather before, but now that she was here with him, she couldn't help but be a little intrigued. After all, they were so far out in the middle of BFE that Brian was now practically the last man left on Earth, as far as Carissa was concerned.

She followed Brian up the steps and through the front door. The inside of the cabin was just as rustic as the outside, and Carissa wondered just how much of the place was actually finished. The main room was huge, with a cathedral ceiling that reached to the top floor. A massive stone fireplace dominated one wall, and a kitchen opened off the back. There were doors on either side that Carissa guessed must lead to bedrooms.

"Let's go, let's go, I ain't got all day," Brian barked, leading Carissa through the main room and up a set of stairs at the back of the house. The second floor was a loft that overlooked the first, and the view from the big windows on the front and back walls was breathtaking. The afternoon sunlight slanted through the trees and threw long shadows across the cabin, and the scent of the forest filled the air.

"You'll stay up here," Brian said, pointing to a door on the left side of the loft.

"This is like, practically a closet!" Carissa pouted as she took the space in. It was smaller than her bathroom back home, barely large enough for the twin bed pushed into one corner and the small dresser against the other wall.

"And what did you expect?" Brian asked, folding his arms over his chest.

Carissa shrugged. "I mean, a place like this, it's gotta have, like, a bunch of rooms, right? Why can't I have a better room? I bet you don't sleep in a closet."

Brian's face reddened, and he looked like he was about to explode. He clenched his fists, and for a moment, Carissa was genuinely afraid that he was going to hit her. She cowered, covering her head with her arms, but then Brian let out a long breath.

"Listen, you little brat," he said, his voice shaking with fury. "I am letting you stay here out of the kindness of my heart. You can either take this room or the shed out back. Or, if you prefer, I can drive you back to the nearest town and you can figure things out on your own."

Carissa shuddered. After she'd left home for college six months prior, Brian had sold the house where she'd grown up and pursued his lifelong dream of becoming a recluse up on this mountain. This cabin was bad, but the town she'd arrived in where he had picked her up was worse. It seemed to be filled with weird old guys like Brian, but unlike Brian, the men Carissa had seen in town didn't seem very concerned with her wellbeing.

Now, Brian lived alone in this remote cabin, and Carissa could only imagine how lonely it must be for him. She hadn't seen a single woman in that town.

"Fine," she muttered.

Brian nodded. "Fine, indeed. Now get unpacked. I've got dinner to make."

"Wait," Carissa said, an idea forming in her head. "You're cooking?"

Brian snorted. "Don't act so shocked. I've been taking care of myself for a long time now. I don't need a princess to tell me what to do."

"Princess?" Carissa repeated, putting her hands on her hips. "Look, I'll have you know that I'm a queen. I don't work. I don't have a job. I don't even have a fucking car. I am a little more than a goddamned princess."

"And you're also still living under my roof, and don't forget that," Brian snapped. "Now, you can either help with dinner, or you can start cleaning. That bathroom over there could use a good scrub," Brian gestured.

Carissa's eyes nearly popped from her head. "A good scrub?!? What do you think'--"

"Oh," Brian laughed. "I'm sorry Queenie. Did you think you'd be living here for free? Aw. Did the poor little Queen think that Daddy was going to swoop in and save her again after she got caught cheating on her exam?"

Carissa blushed. "I didn't cheat," she mumbled.

Brian shrugged. "Doesn't really matter now, does it? Your college expelled you. Your friends dropped you. You've got nothing going for you, and the only thing you've got left is me. Now get yourself changed into something appropriate and come downstairs when you're ready for supper."

Carissa watched as her stepfather turned and stomped down the stairs. She waited until he was gone before throwing herself onto her tiny bed and sobbing.

The cabin was cold. Brian was an asshole. And Carissa wasn't sure how she was going to last here.

She pulled herself up and wiped away her tears. The worst part of all of this was that Brian was right.

Her college had expelled her for cheating, and her friends had dropped her like a hot potato when the news broke. When Carissa's mother had passed away, Brian had always been the one there for her. He'd paid for her tuition, bought her a car, and paid the bills while she studied. But then, she'd screwed up.

Brian's words echoed in her head. You've got nothing going for you.

A fresh wave of tears came to her eyes, but Carissa held them back.

She took her phone out of her pocket and tried to sooth herself with some scrolling, or maybe a little online shopping, and things went from bad to worse.

No reception.

So not only was she trapped up here on Mount Craptacular with the world's most demanding dad, she was also going to have to survive with no contact to the outside world. No social media. No shopping. No life.

She felt her tears begin to spill over and she looked up at the ceiling, blinking rapidly.

Carissa could hear Brian in the kitchen below her. She took a deep breath and reminded herself that she could get through this.

She rolled off the side of her new bed and unzipped her suitcase, looking for something more appropriate to wear to dinner. The minidress and heels that she'd worn to travel didn't really make sense up on this mountain, but she wasn't really a jeans and flannel type of girl either.

She rifled through the clothes in her back until she settled on a pair of denim shorts so short that they were almost a belt. She pulled the zipper up and fastened the button, then adjusted the small strip of fabric that she liked to call a shirt.

The light pink tank top was thin and barely covered her tits, and Carissa knew that there was no way she would ever be able to wear it out in public locally, not in front of all those men who probably hadn't seen a live woman since the Reagan administration.

That's what made it perfect for this situation.

The only reason she had packed the tiny thing was because she knew that the only thing she'd be doing for the next several months was lounging around Brian's cabin. At least this way, she might get him to be a little more agreeable.

"Carissa," Brian called up the stairs. "Dinner is ready."

"Coming!" Carissa called back.

She stood up and the thin, tight fabric of her shorts created a friction against her sensitive, shaved skin that made her blood race through her veins directly into her pussy.

The sensation was so intense that it caught Carissa off guard. She had to put her hands on the wall and lean over to catch her breath.

"Carissa!" Brian's voice boomed up the stairs.

"Yes, Daddy, I'm coming!" she panted back.

She grabbed a hair tie from the top of the dresser and gathered her hair up into a ponytail. She was feeling the heat in the small cabin, and if she wasn't careful, she was going to sweat right through her top.

A drop of perspiration snuck past her collar and slid down between her breasts, and Carissa felt it slide all the way down. She shuddered as her nipples grew taut beneath the thin fabric of her top, and she could see the dark circles clearly outlined against the bright pink.

She turned away from the mirror and walked to the top of the stairs. Brian was waiting for her at the bottom.

"About time," he said. "Now get your ass down here."

"Yes, Daddy," Carissa replied. She took her first step down and felt the thin fabric of her shorts ride up even higher on her legs. They were so short that there was no way they could stay in place.

As she walked down the stairs, the tight fabric crept up further and further, until the front of Carissa's shorts practically disappeared between her legs, revealing the tiny pink thong she'd bought specifically for this trip.

Carissa held her breath and paused on the third step. If she moved another step down, her shorts would disappear completely and her ass would be on full display for her stepfather.

Brian stared at her with his hands on his hips. His gaze swept up and down her body, lingering for a moment on the thin strip of thong that was peeping out from between Carissa's thighs.

"Keep moving, Carissa," Brian said.

Carissa let out the breath that she'd been holding.

"Daddy, I don't know if I should," she whispered. "My clothes are too small. I can't move."

"Do it," Brian replied. "Or I will come up there and punish you."

Carissa knew that Brian meant it. She stepped down, feeling the tight fabric of her shorts slip between her cheeks and disappear. Suddenly, she wasn't feeling so confident about her plan to manipulate Brian. She'd assumed that her stepfather would be flustered when he saw her prancing around practically nude, but Brian didn't seem phased at all. In fact, he seemed to be enjoying himself.

"That's better," Brian said with a nod as Carissa reached the bottom of the stairs. "Now come on over here and help me set the table."

Carissa followed Brian into the kitchen and helped him carry over the food. He had grilled a pair of huge steaks and served them with baked potatoes, a simple salad, and a bottle of red wine. Not exactly haute cuisine, but Carissa was impressed by how well-prepared everything looked.

"You've been holding out on me, Daddy," she said, taking her place at the small table that Brian had set up in front of the big windows.

"And you, little girl," Brian leaned across the table toward Carissa, "have been holding out on me."

Carissa froze in place, a bite of steak pierced on the end of her fork hovering between the two of them.

"What do you mean?" she whispered.

"You're a real looker, aren't you?" Brian said with a smirk. "I'm starting to understand why you got yourself kicked out of college. No man would be able to focus on his studies if you were around."

Carissa blushed and dropped her eyes back to her plate. "Thanks, I guess," she murmured, and popped the bite of steak into her mouth.

The two ate in silence for several minutes, until Carissa's shorts started to make themselves known again. The tight fabric was so small that they barely covered her, and the combination of the fabric rubbing against her body and the way her stepfather's eyes were constantly on her made Carissa's skin tingle. She shifted in her seat, trying to get comfortable, but the sensations only grew more intense.

"Now I think it's about time," Brian studied Carissa's chest, which she'd suddenly become painfully aware of, "that we discuss payment."

"Payment?" Carissa squeaked.

"That's right," Brian smirked. "Payment. What did you think, you'd be staying here for free? Come on, Carissa. You're an adult now. All grown up. Isn't that what you were trying to prove when you came bouncing down those stairs dressed like that? What a big girl you are now?"

"I...I....I..." Carissa stammered. Her face was flaming red, and she felt her nipples harden beneath the thin fabric of her top as Brian stared at her.

"Well," Brian asked. "Do you have a job? Any money saved up from school?"

Carissa shook her head. "I don't even have a car anymore."

"I know," Brian snorted. "And you don't even know how to drive one."

"Daddy!" Carissa protested.

Brian held up a hand. "Don't Daddy me. You're eighteen years old and you've never driven a car in your life. Hell, if I had to guess, I'd say you've never even done the laundry, or cleaned a bathroom, or done any sort of work whatsoever, have you?"

Carissa looked down at her plate. "No, Daddy," she whispered.

Brian sat back in his chair and folded his arms across his chest. "I didn't think so. Now, what exactly did you think was going to happen here, Queenie? You don't cook. You don't clean. So," Brian licked his lips, "what do you do?"

Carissa looked up at Brian through her lashes. "I don't know," she said in a small voice. "I was just hoping that you would take care of me like always, Daddy."

"Oh, I'm going to take care of you. Don't you worry. But things aren't going to be like they were when you were a little girl. I'm not going to let you live here for free anymore."

Brian leaned forward across the table and pointed at Carissa. "Now, you're going to be earning your keep around here. And there are going to be some new rules. Do you understand?"

Carissa nodded. "Yes, Daddy. I understand."

"Good." Brian smiled. "Then let's begin."

Carissa watched as Brian stood up and walked to the front door of the cabin. He opened it and a chilly breeze drifted in, making the flames in the fireplace flicker.

"Come here, Carissa," Brian said, beckoning with one finger.

Carissa rose from her seat and walked to the front door. The chill in the air made her nipples harden against the thin fabric of her shirt.

"Do you see that?" Brian pointed out the door toward the forest.

"Yes," Carissa breathed, looking out into the darkness.

"Do you know what it is?"

"No," Carissa whispered.

Brian stepped closer to Carissa and lowered his face next to hers, until his mouth was against her ear. Carissa could feel the warmth of his breath against her skin and her pulse quickened.

"That, my dear," Brian murmured, "is freedom."

Carissa blinked. "What?"

Brian stepped away from her and walked back to the table. "You heard me," he said. "Out there, beyond these walls, you'll have the chance to live your life. To be free."

Carissa looked from Brian to the dark forest.

"You mean..." she began, but her voice trailed off.

"Go on," Brian urged. "Say it. You mean leave? I mean exactly that, Carissa. You can walk out that door and never come back if you want to. You can find a job, a man, a life. Out there."

Brian gestured again toward the woods. "But if you stay here, with me," he said, "you'll have to pay for it."

"I don't understand," Carissa whispered.

Brian shrugged. "It's really quite simple. You've already seen your bedroom. I've got the shed out back that could be converted to a guest room, if needed. I'm a very reasonable man, and I'm sure we can come to some sort of arrangement."

Carissa hesitated. On the one hand, she didn't want to give up so easily. She could survive out there, in the world. She was certain of it. She was beautiful, smart, and driven.

But on the other hand, Carissa had to admit that her life was currently in shambles. She didn't have any money. Or a job. And she didn't even know how to drive a car.

She looked back at Brian, who was watching her expectantly.

"What about school?" she asked. "Can I go back to college?"

Brian shook his head. "No, Queenie. That's not possible. You were kicked out. There's no going back."

"Then how will I get my degree?" Carissa asked. "How will I find a job? A man? A life?"

"That wouldn't really be my problem anymore," Brian replied. "Not if you leave. If you leave, you're on your own. Go ahead. Start walking if you think there's something better out there for you. But if you stay, you're mine."

Carissa thought for a moment. She was used to having everything taken care of for her by others. She'd never been on her own. But now, her mother was gone, she'd been expelled from college, and her friends had abandoned her.

The thought of leaving the safety of Brian's cabin was terrifying. She looked back at her stepfather, and for the first time, she noticed that he was a good-looking man.

"I'm staying," she said quietly.

"Okay. Good girl."

Carissa's ears pricked. Good girl? No one had called her good in a long time. Not since she was little.

"Thank you, Daddy," she whispered.

"You're welcome," Brian replied. "Now, let's go over the rules. First, you will obey me at all times. This is my house, and I make the decisions here. Second, you will always be respectful of me. If I tell you to do something, you will do it without hesitation. Third, and most importantly, you will always put my needs before your own."

Carissa nodded. "Yes, Daddy."

"Good girl. Now, what's your name?"

"Carissa," Carissa said.

"No, not anymore. From now on, your name is Queenie. You are my Queen, and I am your King. Do you understand?"

"Yes, Daddy," Carissa breathed. The thought of being Brian's Queen excited her in a way that she'd never experienced before.

"But I need you to understand," Brian traced his finger around Carissa's nipple and then pinched it until she squealed. "That I'm an absolute ruler. A tyrant, if you will. And the only you're going to exist here with any kind of comfort at all is if you make me happy. Now." Brian hooked his thumb into Carissa's impossibly tight shorts. "Do you know how to make Daddy happy?"

Carissa nodded. "I think so, Daddy."

Brian smiled. "Good girl. Now, get down on your knees."

Carissa obeyed, dropping to her knees in front of her stepfather. Brian undid his pants and pulled his cock out, stroking it in front of Carissa's face. Carissa gasped when she saw the size of it. It was huge, far bigger than any of the boys she'd fooled around with before.

"Open your mouth," Brian commanded.

Carissa parted her lips and Brian pushed his cock between them. She gagged as the head of his cock hit the back of her throat, but she fought through it. She didn't want to disappoint Brian.

"That's it, Queenie, just like that," Brian encouraged. "Now, suck it."

Carissa did as she was told, swirling her tongue around the head of Brian's cock while he groaned with pleasure.

"Show Daddy you know how to suck like a good girl," he growled.

Carissa bobbed her head up and down on Brian's cock, sucking and licking him with abandon. He grabbed a fistful of her hair and guided her movements, using her mouth to pleasure himself. Carissa moaned around Brian's cock as she felt her own pussy growing wet with desire.

"Now take it all," Brian instructed, pressing Carissa's face against his body.

Carissa opened her throat and took all of Brian's cock, swallowing it to the base. It was so big that it filled her completely, and she struggled to breathe around it.

"That's it, Queenie," Brian said, holding Carissa's head in place. "I want you to choke on my cock. Show me that you're a good girl. Suck it like the dirty little whore you are."

Carissa obeyed, sucking and licking Brian's cock like her life depended on it. Because, in a way, it did. Without Brian, she was lost. And Carissa was determined to make Daddy happy, no matter what it took. She was going to show him what a good little girl she could be.

As she continued to suck Brian's cock, he began to thrust his hips, fucking her face with abandon. Carissa gagged and choked, but she kept going, knowing that she had to make Brian feel good.

"That's it, Queenie, take it all. You're a good little slut, aren't you?"

Carissa moaned in response, the vibrations making Brian's cock twitch in her mouth.

"Yes, you are," Brian said. "And now, it's time for you to show me what a good girl you can be." He pulled Carissa's head back by her hair, her red mouth still hanging open from the girth of his cock, drool covering her chin. "Take off that slutty little outfit."

Carissa obeyed, stripping off her clothes until she was completely naked. She stood there in front of Brian, shivering from the cold, her nipples hard and her pussy glistening with desire.

Brian walked around her, appraising her body. "You're a very pretty girl, Queenie," he said. "But you need to learn that being pretty isn't enough. You've got to know how to please a man, too." He stepped behind Carissa and smacked her ass hard. "Get on your hands and knees. Right here on the floor. Show me that you're a good girl."

Carissa dropped to the floor and got on all fours, her ass up in the air. She felt Brian's hands on her hips, pulling her back towards him.

"Now, let's see how much of a good girl you really are," he said, rubbing the head of his cock against Carissa's pussy. "Show me that you can be a good girl for Daddy. Tell me what you are."

"I'm a good girl, Daddy," Carissa said, her voice quivering.

"You're what?" Brian slapped her ass again, leaving a red mark on her pale skin.

"I'm a good girl, Daddy!" Carissa repeated.

"And what does a good girl deserve?" Brian asked, teasing Carissa with his cock.

"A good fucking, Daddy," Carissa breathed, her pussy aching with desire.

Brian laughed. "That's right. And that's exactly what you're going to get." He pushed the head of his cock into Carissa's pussy, stretching her tight opening. "Because you're Daddy's good little slut, aren't you?"

"Yes, Daddy," Carissa moaned as Brian filled her up, his cock pulsing inside of her.

"Say it!" Brian commanded. "Tell me what you are!"

"I'm Daddy's good little slut!" Carissa cried out, the sensation of Brian's cock inside of her pushing her over the edge.

Carissa heard the sound of Brian spit and before she had time to react she felt his wet thumb pressing in circles around her tight asshole.

"Daddy," she started, but then Brian's thumb was inside her asshole, and it was too late. She screamed out as he stretched her open, pushing her boundaries as he fucked her pussy and her ass at the same time.

"That's right, Queenie," Brian groaned. "You're my little whore. You're mine to do whatever I want with. And I'm going to show you what it means to be a good girl. I'm going to fuck you until you can't walk, and then I'm going to fuck you some more."

Carissa gasped as Brian spanked her ass hard, the sting of his hand only heightening the pleasure of his cock inside of her.

"Do you like that, Queenie?" Brian asked, spanking her again.

"Yes, Daddy!" Carissa moaned. "Please, please fuck me, Daddy. Please show me what a good girl I can be."

Brian obliged, fucking Carissa's pussy and her ass hard, pounding into her relentlessly. He held her hips in place, using her body for his own pleasure.

"You're my little slut, aren't you, Queenie?" Brian grunted, spanking her ass again.

"Yes, Daddy!" Carissa cried out, her pleasure mounting with each thrust of Brian's cock.

"Say it," Brian growled, spanking her ass again. "Say you're my little slut."

"I'm your little slut, Daddy!" Carissa screamed as her orgasm overtook her, her body shaking with pleasure.

Brian continued to fuck her, his cock pulsing inside of her pussy. "That's right," he said. "You're my little slut. You're my Queen. And I'm going to show you what it means to be a good girl."

He pulled out of her pussy and pushed the head of his cock against her asshole. Carissa gasped as he stretched her open, filling her ass with his massive cock.

"Fuck, you're tight," Brian grunted as he began to pound her ass, spanking it with each thrust of his hips.

"Yes, Daddy, please," Carissa begged. "Please fuck me, Daddy. Please show me what a good girl I can be."

Brian grabbed Carissa's hair and pulled her head back as he fucked her ass, spanking her with each thrust.

"You're such a good girl, Queenie," he said. "And you're all mine."

Carissa moaned as the pleasure built within her, her body trembling with desire. Brian's cock stretched her open, filling her completely.

"I want you to cum in my ass, Daddy," she begged. "Please, Daddy, cum in my ass. Show me what a good girl I can be."

Brian groaned as he came inside of Carissa's ass, his cock pulsing as he shot his load deep inside of her.

"That's it, Queenie, take it all. You're my good little slut, aren't you?"

"Yes, Daddy!" Carissa cried out as another orgasm washed over her. "I'm your good little slut. I'm yours!"

Brian pulled his cock out of Carissa's ass and smacked her ass one last time. "Good girl," he said. "Now spread your cheeks and show me how Daddy wrecked your tight little asshole."

Carissa felt her cheeks burn as she obeyed and a dribble of cum came out of her body and dripped down her thigh.

Brian chuckled and shook his head. "What a little whore," he said, and then turned and walked away, leaving Carissa panting on the floor of the cabin.

Carissa watched Brian's retreating form, her mind racing with the events that had just occurred. She was still on all fours, her ass in the air, Brian's cum dripping from her body. She had never experienced anything like that before.

She felt a mix of shame and excitement, and she knew that she would do anything for Brian. She sat back on her haunches and thought about what had happened.

Brian's dominance had been intoxicating, and she knew that she wanted more. She couldn't wait to be his Queen, to be his little slut, to be Daddy's good girl.

* * *

DADDY'S FORBIDDEN GADGET

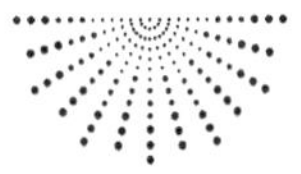

* * *

"You don't think your stepdad is going to be mad?"

"Rick?" Madison laughed. "Yeah right. I have him wrapped around my little finger."

Plus, Madison thought to herself, if we get back before he gets off work, what Daddy doesn't know won't hurt him.

The truth was, Maddie knew, if Rick found out that she'd taken his old Mustang out joyriding with her bestie Taylor, he would absolutely blow a gasket. This car was his baby, and Maddie couldn't blame him. It was sweet, cherry red, with black leather interior, and a souped-up engine that made it purr like a cat in heat. She knew he'd spent a fortune on the rebuild, and he only drove it on weekends, so that it wouldn't get scratched. It was his pride and joy, and he'd never have let her take it if she had asked.

That was why she and Taylor had made sure he was long gone by the time they came down and took it out of the garage.

Maddie thought back to a couple hours ago, when she had come downstairs from her room and found her stepdad loading his briefcase in the kitchen. She had been wearing nothing but a small blue robe, and she liked the way Rick's eyes lingered on her as she crossed the room. Ever since her mom had run off with the pool boy two years ago, things between them had grown a little more... intimate. It had all started one night when Rick got drunk, and Maddie had to help him up to his room. He'd been too incoherent to make it on his own, and when they got to his bedroom, Maddie had been surprised by how strong he was. He'd picked her up like she weighed nothing at all, and carried her to bed. Then he'd thanked her for taking such good care of him, and untied her robe before slipping it off her shoulders.

She hadn't protested when he kissed her, or when he bent down and took her nipple in his mouth.

Rick was a handsome guy, tall and muscular with a nice face and short greying hair. He wore a suit to work every day, and he had a good job managing a bank. The only thing that seemed to be missing from his life was someone to love him. And since her mom had been gone for so long, Maddie figured she could provide some of the companionship he was missing. After all, he'd been taking care of her since she was a little girl. It was the least she could do for him.

So she'd let him pull the sheets back and climb on top of her. Unfortunately for her that night, Rick had come to his senses before things escalated. He stopped just short of actually having sex with her, and promised that it would never happen again.

But Maddie had been more than ready for him that night, and she knew she wouldn't turn him away if he ever decided to come back for more.

She thought about the way his cock must look beneath those dress pants, and she imagined how it would feel in her hand. She wondered if it was big or small, if it would taste like the others she had taken into her mouth. And she wondered if he would be rough with her, or gentle.

She wondered if it would hurt the first time.

Maddie blushed at the memory. She knew she was getting herself all worked up, and she pushed the thought from her mind as she turned on the radio. Rick was hot, but he was also such an asshole. He never let her drive his car and he'd been nagging her to either get a job or sign up for some classes at the local community college ever since she had graduated. That's why she didn't feel bad about stealing his car for the day.

Well, not stealing. Not technically. Borrowing was more like it. Besides, it wasn't as if he ever took her anywhere anyway. He was always too busy with work. So she figured she was entitled to a little fun now and then.

She looked in the rear view mirror again.

"Shit."

"What is it?" Taylor asked, pulling the magazine away from her face. "Why are we slowing down? We aren't back already, are we?"

"Nope," Maddie said. "I think that cop wants us to pull over."

A moment later the police cruiser on their ass had it's lights on and blared the siren. Maddie could already feel a sweat prickle on the back of her neck as she sank down into the driver's seat.

Fuck! It was a lady cop. There went her plan to try to flirt her way out of a ticket.

"License and registration please," the cop said, once she had gotten out and presented herself at the window. She was tall, with blonde hair pulled back into a ponytail. She looked young, maybe around the same age as Maddie's stepdad. And, like Maddie's stepdad, she looked like a total hardass.

"Here," Maddie handed over her papers. "But I wasn't actually--"

"Whose car is this," the cop demanded before Maddie could try to present her case. "This registration says Rick Parker and your license says Madison Nelson."

"It's my dad's," Maddie explained.

"The addresses are different."

"Oh," Madison cringed. "I moved out for a couple months after I graduated but I moved back."

"I'm going to have to run this," the cop shook her head.

"No!" Maddie started. "It's my dad's I swear. He let me borrow it."

"This car was reported stolen," the cop shot back. I'm going to have to ask you to step out of the vehicle, Ma'am. You too," she indicated Taylor.

"No!" Madison cried. "It's my dad's just let me call him! He can explain everything!"

"Ma'am, out of the car."

Maddie felt a rush of panic, her mind racing for a way out of this. What was she going to tell Rick when he found out that she was the one who took his precious car? He was going to kill her. He would be so pissed, she'd probably be grounded for life.

"Please," Maddie begged. "I'm sorry! Just let me call my dad. I'm sure he's not mad that I took it anymore, I'm sure he just forgot to tell you guys."

"Fine," the cop rolled her eyes. "One phone call. Hurry it up."

"Thank you," Maddie said. She was already pulling her phone out of her pocket. It was her only hope. She prayed that Rick would answer the phone.

"Hello?" his gruff voice answered on the third ring.

"Daddy," Maddie said, trying to sound as sweet as possible.

"Maddie? What the fuck? Is that you?" Rick asked.

"Um, yeah," Maddie started, "it's me. Listen, I'm really sorry I took your car without asking but Taylor and I just needed to get out and do some shopping and I was in a hurry and I thought you wouldn't mind if I borrowed it for a little while, so I just--"

"Where are you?" Rick cut in, his tone impatient.

"I'm at the gas station on 5th, by the mall."

"Fine. Drop your friend off and then come straight home. Put the cop on the phone."

Maddie waited with baited breath as the cop clarified with her stepfather that it was all a big misunderstanding and the car wasn't actually stolen.

"Hmph," the cop shook her head as she handed the phone back to Madison. "You might have been better off having me take you in. He sounds pissed."

"Um," Madison swallowed. "What should I do now?"

"You heard him. Get your butt home," the cop said. "And don't let me catch you speeding again."

Madison dropped her friend Taylor off and briefly considered not going home at all. Maybe she should just keep driving. Maybe she should turn herself in to the cop for stealing Rick's car. At least they would feed her three meals a day in jail.

But she knew that Rick would call the cops and get her out eventually, and that would make him even madder. So she headed home. She'd only made it a few blocks when her phone rang.

"Hello?" she said into the speaker, still a little afraid.

"Get your ass in the house," Rick told her.

"I'm almost there."

"Good. I'll be waiting."

By the time Madison pulled into the garage she was sweating like a whore in church. Her heart was pounding in her chest, and her legs felt weak when she stepped out of the car.

Rick was standing in the doorway that led to the kitchen, his arms crossed over his chest. He was wearing a nice blue suit and he looked very handsome, his broad shoulders filling out the jacket perfectly. But his face was grim, his eyes narrowed.

"Uh, hi," Maddie started.

"Hi?" Rick shook his head. "I ought to tear your ass up for that. You think you're a big shot huh? Sneak out in my car?"

"I'm sorry," Maddie started. "I just thought--"

"Well you thought wrong."

"I won't do it again I promise!"

"Damn right you won't," Rick growled. "You know what I had to go through today? I had to leave work early to go down to the station to tell them to let you go. Do you know how busy I am? Do you have any idea how many important things I have going on?"

"I'm sorry," Maddie said again, her voice small. She could feel tears stinging her eyes. She hadn't meant to make him this upset, she just wanted to get out of the house for a little while.

"You're damn right you're sorry. Now get your ass upstairs."

"What?"

"You heard me. Now."

Maddie gulped and hurried past her stepdad into the kitchen. He followed her through the door, then watched her as she started up the stairs.

"Take your clothes off," he commanded.

"What?"

"You heard me. I want to make sure you're not stealing any of my shit. Take your clothes off."

Maddie felt her face turn hot with a mixture of shame and anger. The way Rick was looking at her made her feel naked already, but she did as he asked. She was too afraid not to. She reached behind her and unzipped her shorts, then pushed them down over her legs and stepped out of them. Next she peeled off her top, and she could feel Rick's eyes on her as she stood up to face him in just her bra and panties.

"All of it," he growled.

She looked away from his piercing gaze and reached behind her back to unclasp her bra, letting it fall down her arms and onto the carpet. Her nipples were rock hard and her face was red with embarrassment. She knew Rick was staring at her body, and it made her feel ashamed and exposed. She had to use her hands to cover her tits, and she turned sideways so he couldn't see her panties.

"Now take those off," he told her, his eyes narrowing.

Maddie hooked her fingers into the waistband of her panties and pulled them down slowly. Her pussy was completely bare, her slit swollen and wet with excitement. She tried to keep her legs pressed together, but she wasn't fast enough to hide what Rick had already seen.

"So you like that huh?" he asked her, pointing at her pussy.

Maddie didn't answer. She kept her head down, staring at the floor.

"Go to your room and wait for me there," Rick said.

She turned away from him and hurried upstairs, her heart racing in her chest. She heard him coming up behind her and she hurried into her room, pulling the door closed behind her. She briefly considered putting on more clothes, but she didn't dare to provoke Rick any further. She had never seen him this angry before.

She stood with her back against the door, breathing hard. She was still completely naked, her nipples hard and her pussy aching for attention.

What was Rick going to do to her? Was he really that mad? He'd never hit her before, but she wasn't sure what to expect now that she had gotten herself in this situation. She wasn't even sure how to feel about it. She was ashamed to be seen naked by her stepdad, but there was something else going on. A sort of excitement that she couldn't quite explain. She was afraid, but she was also horny. She wanted to run, but she also wanted to see what Rick was going to do next.

After a few minutes she heard him coming down the hall. She jumped back from the door and climbed onto her bed, wrapping the sheets around her naked body.

Rick walked in, closed the door behind him, and leaned against the wall. He had a beer in his hand and he was looking at her, his eyes roaming over her body. Maddie looked away, too ashamed to make eye contact.

"I'm sorry Daddy," she said, her voice barely a whisper.

"Sorry?" Rick shook his head. "That's not good enough. I think you need to be punished."

"Please," Madison begged. "I won't do it again I promise!"

"I know you won't," Rick told her. "Because I'm going to teach you a lesson you'll never forget."

Maddie looked up at him then, her eyes wide. She saw that he was loosening his tie, pulling it off and letting it fall to the floor. Her heart started beating faster when he unbuttoned the top of his shirt, and her breath caught in her throat as he reached down and unbuckled his belt.

"Get up, turn around, and put your hands flat on your desk," he commanded.

"W-what?" Maddie asked, shocked by the request.

"You heard me. Get up! And leave that sheet on the bed."

Maddie's mind raced with the possibilities. Was he really going to punish her like a child? Like a little girl who had misbehaved? Was he going to spank her?

She felt a rush of fear, but it was accompanied by something else. A strange, tingling excitement that she couldn't explain. She'd never been spanked before, but she'd always wondered what it might be like. She couldn't deny that she was a little intrigued.

"Daddy, please," she started, but Rick cut her off with a wave of his hand.

"Don't 'Daddy' me. I've done everything for you, and this is how you repay me? Stealing my fucking car? That's the last time you're ever going to disobey me."

"Okay," Maddie nodded, tears in her eyes. "I'll do better, I swear."

"No," Rick shook his head. "You won't. Now get your ass up and over there before you make me any angrier."

Maddie climbed off the bed and crossed the room, feeling her stepfather's eyes on her every step of the way. She bent over in front of her desk and pressed her palms flat against the top of it.

"Now turn your toes in toward each other and spread your heels out," Rick told her.

"But..."

"Do it now."

Maddie swallowed hard and spread her feet apart. She could feel the cool air from the air conditioner on her wet lips and then she knew for sure that Rick could see everything.

"That's better," he said.

She felt him approach behind her, and she shivered when he placed his hand on the small of her back.

"Please don't do this," she begged, but her plea was ignored.

She felt Rick's fingers brush against her pussy and she cried out in surprise. His hand was warm and rough, and it felt so good against her smooth, sensitive lips. She couldn't believe what she was feeling. Her own stepdad touching her like this.

"So you like this huh?" Rick asked her, running his fingers up and down her slit. "I can see that you're wet already. I can tell how much you want it."

"Daddy," Maddie started, but she stopped short when he reached up and grabbed a handful of her hair.

"Tell Daddy what you want."

"I want... I want you to..." Maddie blushed, unable to finish the sentence.

"What?" Rick growled, bending his head down to her ear. "Tell me what you want me to do."

"Please," Maddie begged.

Rick reached up and grabbed the back of her neck, pushing her head down so that her cheek was pressed against the cool wood of her desk.

"Tell me what you want me to do!"

"Fuck me!" she cried out. "Please! Fuck me!"

Rick let out a low laugh and grabbed Maddie's wrist, forcing her hand onto the bulge of his pants. She reached down and felt his cock, long and hard beneath his suit. She knew exactly what she wanted to do with it, but she didn't dare move without permission.

"Is that what you want?" Rick growled. "You want Daddy's cock?"

"Yes!" Maddie cried. "Oh please, Daddy!"

"Beg me," Rick commanded.

"Please Daddy, I need your cock. I need it!"

"This cock is only for good girls, Madison. Tell me. Are you a good girl?"

"I'm sorry, I'm so sorry! I'll be good! Please!"

"You'll be good?" Rick asked. "You promise?"

"I swear!" Maddie begged. "Just please fuck me!"

"I think it's too late for promises, Madison. You're not a good girl. In fact, I think it's time you accepted your punishment."

Madison gasped as she heard her stepfather slip his belt from the loops on his pants. She could picture it in her mind, the leather slipping through the metal buckle, and the soft clank as it hit the floor.

Then she felt the leather against her skin, the sting of it as it struck her ass.

"Ow!" Maddie cried. "Please!"

"Quiet," Rick growled.

"But it hurts!" Maddie cried. "Please stop!"

"Bad girls get punished."

He spanked her again, and this time the pain was sharp and hot. She could feel the leather of the belt against her flesh, and she knew it was leaving a mark. Tears came to her eyes and she tried to stand, but Rick pressed her back against the desk.

"What did I say?" he demanded. "If you move, it will only get worse."

She felt the leather come down on her ass again, and this time she screamed out loud. It hurt more than anything she had ever felt before. But underneath the pain was a strange tingling sensation that she couldn't ignore. Her pussy was throbbing, aching for attention. The pain and pleasure mingled together into something new, something exciting. She couldn't tell one from the other anymore, and she realized that she wanted more.

"Please," she begged. "More!"

Rick brought the belt down again, harder this time. She could feel the sting of it on her ass, but she also felt a rush of pleasure between her legs.

"Yes!" she cried. "More!"

"You like that?" Rick asked her, bringing the belt down on her again. "You like getting punished?"

"Yes!"

He brought the belt down again, this time a little lower. She felt the leather strike the top of her thigh, and she cried out in pain and pleasure.

"Do you want Daddy to stop?" Rick asked her.

"No!" Maddie cried. "Please, I want more!"

"Then beg for it," Rick demanded.

"Please, Daddy. Please spank me again."

Rick brought the belt down on her again, this time even harder. The pain was so intense that she thought she might pass out. Her vision went blurry and she felt her knees grow weak.

"Are you going to behave for Daddy now?" Rick demanded, stroking the burning skin of Madison's tender ass.

"Yes, Daddy," she whimpered.

"Good. Now stand up and get on your bed."

Madison stood up on shaky legs, and climbed onto her bed. Rick grabbed her arm and pulled her back down so that she was sitting on the edge of the mattress. He grabbed her by the back of her neck and pulled her head down until her face was in front of his cock.

"Now open up," he commanded.

Maddie obeyed, her lips parting to take him inside. She felt his cock slide across her tongue and she closed her lips around him, sucking him in deep. The taste of him was intoxicating, the feel of his hard flesh in her mouth making her head swim with desire.

She looked up at him, her eyes wide as she took him deeper. She saw the pleasure on his face, the look of lust in his eyes, and it made her want him even more. She wanted to make him feel good, to give him everything he wanted.

She sucked him deep, taking him all the way down her throat. He groaned in pleasure, grabbing a handful of her hair and pulling her closer. She felt his cock twitch in her mouth as he reached his limit, and she knew he was close.

"That's it, baby," he groaned. "Suck it."

She did as he asked, her lips wrapped tightly around his cock. She could feel his balls tighten up and she knew he was about to come. She wanted it, craved it.

She sucked him hard, taking him as deep as she could.

Rick let out a low growl and pulled his cock from Madison's mouth, staring down at her tear-streaked face.

"Turn around and get on your hands and knees," Rick ordered. "Show Daddy your pretty red ass again."

Madison turned around and got on her hands and knees, presenting her ass to her stepfather. She felt his hands on her hips, his fingers digging into her skin.

"Beg me for it," Rick commanded.

"Please," Maddie begged. "Please fuck me, Daddy."

Rick let out a low growl as he thrust his hips forward, burying his cock inside Madison's tight pussy. She gasped as he entered her, her body stretching to accommodate his girth. She was so wet, so ready for him that he slid in easily. She could feel her muscles clenching around him, her body begging for more.

He pulled back slowly, then thrust forward again, his cock sliding in and out of her with ease. She moaned as he filled her, his cock hitting just the right spot inside her. She felt him lean over her, his chest pressed against her back. His breath was hot in her ear and she could feel his heartbeat pounding in his chest.

"You like that?" he whispered, his voice low and rough. "You like getting fucked by Daddy?"

"Yes," Maddie moaned.

"Say it," he growled. "Tell Daddy how much you love his cock."

"I love your cock," she cried. "I love it, Daddy."

Rick's hands moved up to her breasts, his fingers finding her nipples. He pinched them between his thumbs and forefingers, rolling them gently. The sensation was incredible, sending shockwaves of pleasure through her entire body. She could feel her pussy getting wetter and wetter, her muscles tightening around his cock as he pumped into her.

"Oh god," she moaned. "Daddy, I'm going to come!"

Rick's hands moved back down to her hips, gripping her tightly. His fingers dug into her flesh as he fucked her harder and faster.

"Be a good girl and come for Daddy, then," he growled, thrusting deep inside her.

She felt his cock swell inside her as he reached his limit, his fingers tightening around her hips as he came. She cried out as her own orgasm hit, her body trembling as pleasure washed over her. She felt his cock pulsing inside her as he came, his cum filling her pussy.

Rick pulled out and collapsed on the bed next to her, breathing hard. She rolled over to face him, her eyes wide and her cheeks flushed with excitement.

"You're not mad at me anymore, are you?" Maddie asked, looking up at her stepdad hopefully.

Rick laughed and shook his head. "No, baby. Daddy's not mad anymore."

"I promise I won't take your car without asking again," she said, leaning down to kiss his chest.

Rick wrapped his arm around her and pulled her close, planting a kiss on the top of her head. "Good girl," he told her.

"Does this mean I can borrow the car again?" she asked, looking up at him with a mischievous grin.

Rick let out a low growl and rolled on top of her, pinning her to the bed. "I think you've been punished enough for one night. But don't push your luck."

Maddie giggled and wrapped her arms around him, pulling him in for another kiss.

"I love you, Daddy," she whispered.

Rick smiled and kissed her softly on the lips. "I love you too, baby girl."

Maddie snuggled up against his chest, feeling safe and content. She knew that she was in for another round of punishment if Rick ever found out what she and Taylor had really done in the backseat of his Mustang. But she wasn't worried about it. She knew her Daddy would forgive her. He always did.

And besides, she thought, it was totally worth it.

TAKING CARE OF DADDY

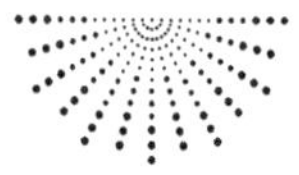

* * *

"Are you sure this is okay?" Jessa put her bags down next to the bed in her former stepfather's guest room, looking around with uncertainty.

"Jess, I know that your mother and I don't really see eye to eye anymore, but I wasn't going to let you sleep in a damn car. Especially not that old hatchback."

"Thanks, Jon," Jessa said, and then immediately felt stupid. What was the right way to address your ex-stepdad, especially after years of calling him "Dad"? "I appreciate it."

"It's no problem. You'll always have a home here, you know." Jon shrugged. "You need to use the bathroom? There's one just across the hall. I'll go get some sheets for the bed."

He disappeared out the door, and Jessa looked around the room. She'd always called this place "her house", even after her mom had divorced her stepfather, and she still considered it a safe space. Still, things were different now. Her mother had walked out on Jon when a new guy caught her eye, but Jessa had never expected her mother to treat her with the same callous disregard. But her mom had a new boy toy, and this new boy was closer to Jessa's age than her mother's. One too many friendly comments from her mom's new boyfriend, and Jessa had found herself out on her ass with barely a penny to her name.

"It's not going to be like last time, you little bitch," her mom had screamed. "Get out and don't come back. You've been nothing but a drain since your father left."

Jessa's dad had been gone for over a decade, and had never provided more than the occasional postcard or Christmas gift. She hadn't been all that surprised to find that he was the least of her worries.

She heard Jon moving around the hall, making the bed up with sheets. "Hey, um...thanks, Dad."

The rustling sounds paused, and she wondered if she'd said the wrong thing. "It's nothing, Jess," he said, and she knew he was smiling.

"So," she said, walking out into the hall and leaning against the doorframe, watching him smooth out the bedspread. "How've you been doing? It's been awhile since we talked."

"Things are pretty good." He sat down on the bed, stretching his arms above his head. "Business is going well. We've got a few new guys that I'm training, and they're coming along nicely."

Jessa nodded. Her stepfather—former stepfather?—had always worked in security. It was a job he was good at, and he had the physique to prove it. The man was built, with wide shoulders and strong arms that she had always associated with safety and stability. He kept himself in great shape. She had a flash of a memory, watching her stepfather lift heavy pieces of furniture as he helped her clean out her bedroom, packing her things up into cardboard boxes.

"How's your mom doing?" Jon asked, and she realized she'd been staring.

"She's okay," Jessa said, feeling awkward. "Well, better than okay, I guess. She's really happy with her new boyfriend."

Jon gave her a rueful smile. "That's good. I'm glad to hear it. I'm not holding any hard feelings toward her. Sometimes these things just don't work out, that's all."

"I'm sorry." She looked at her feet.

"What? Hey, you don't have anything to be sorry about. Come here, Jess."

She went and sat on the bed next to him, and he put his arm around her, pulling her close. It felt nice. Jon had always been the best thing about her life, and it felt so comfortable to sit here, close to him, and feel like things were okay.

"I'm not sorry because of your and Mom's divorce," she said, her face against his chest. She could feel his heartbeat, a steady thump under his thin t-shirt. "I mean, I am sorry, but..."

"It's okay. I know what you mean. Your mom and I weren't working out for a while. It's not your fault."

"But I'm still sorry that things turned out like this," she said. "It's not fair."

Jon chuckled. "Sometimes life's not fair. How's the bed? Do you need more blankets? Pillows?"

"No, it's fine," Jessa said. She sat up, and saw that Jon's blue eyes were focused on her face.

"Good," he said. "You know, Jess, if you ever need anything, just let me know. Even if it's just a place to stay. You're always welcome here."

"Thanks, Dad." She smiled. "It's funny. Even though I'm not a kid anymore, it's still nice to know that."

"You know," Jon's eyes travelled over Jessa's body in a way that made her heart flutter, "you're looking pretty thin. Have you been eating right?"

"Yeah, I'm fine. Just not that hungry these days."

"You need some meat on those bones." His eyes rested on her chest, where her breasts pressed out against the fabric of her shirt. "You should eat more."

She flushed, not sure how to respond. The look in her stepfather's eyes was so intense, so different from the usual friendly glances she was used to. It made her nervous. But there was something else, too. A warmth spreading through her chest, a strange tension building between her legs. She looked away.

"I should fix some supper for us. Why don't you take a shower and then come meet me downstairs and we'll have a nice meal?"

"Okay, Dad," Jessa said.

"You're welcome, sweetheart," he said, patting her thigh before he stood up. His hand rested for just a moment on the curve of her leg, and she could swear that his fingers lingered for longer than was necessary.

Jessa turned on the hot water in her bathroom and stripped out of the clothes she'd been wearing for three days before she broke down and asked Jon if she could temporarily stay with him while she tried to get on her feet. Her skin was covered in a thin sheen of sweat, and there was a layer of dirt ground into her hair and skin. She stepped into the shower and closed the curtain behind her.

As the hot water hit her body, she sighed. This was just what she needed. For a moment, she felt almost like a kid again, coming home from a day at school.

She scrubbed shampoo into her dark hair, and watched the suds slide over her pale body and pool at her feet. As the heat from the water washed over her, she found her thoughts drifting back to the way

Jon's eyes had rested on her body, and the firm grip of his hand on her leg. It was an unfamiliar feeling, the way her body had responded.

"Ugh, what's wrong with me?" Jessa whispered.

It was disgusting, thinking about her stepfather like that. And yet she couldn't deny the growing heat between her thighs, and the flush spreading over her chest. She closed her eyes and tried to picture Jon's face, his strong jaw, his muscular body, and the strange feelings only intensified. She was ashamed of herself, but there was no denying the truth.

Her stepfather turned her on.

She couldn't go downstairs and face him like this. She needed to get her head straight. Jessa took the handheld showerhead from it's mount and turned the setting to pulse. She let the water beat her shoulders, then her breasts before moving the stream down between her legs.

"Ah..."

As the water massaged her pussy, Jessa felt her breathing grow deeper, faster. It had been weeks since she'd masturbated, and she'd never had a need as strong as this. She tried not to think about Jon and his strong hands as the water worked its way over her body, but it was no use. Her mind was full of him, the memory of his touch, his scent.

She moaned softly and pressed the showerhead harder against her clit, feeling the throbbing waves of pleasure build as the water worked it's way inside her. As her legs trembled, she reached out and steadied herself against the wall, and closed her eyes.

"Oh...god..."

With a sudden gasp, she came, her whole body shaking as the orgasm rocked her.

"Jon!" she let out an involuntary cry as she climaxed, her knees buckling under her. She leaned back against the wall and slid down until she was sitting on the floor of the tub, panting and spent.

"Everything okay in there?"

Jessa nearly died of embarrassment at the knock on the door. Jon was right outside.

"Y-yeah, everything's fine," she said, trying to keep her voice calm. "Sorry. Just slipped."

"All right. I thought I heard you call me. Hurry up and finish getting cleaned up, you don't want your food to get cold."

"Okay." Jessa swallowed. "Sorry. Be out in a few."

After she was sure that Jon had gone back downstairs, she stood up on shaking legs and turned off the water. Her whole body felt strange, like there was some electric charge running just under her skin.

"Get a hold of yourself, Jessa," she said aloud.

She toweled off, then pulled on a pair of clean underwear and a wrinkled sundress that she had balled up in her backpack. She wanted to look nice for dinner but this was the best she could do at the moment. She took one last look in the mirror, and smoothed her damp hair, before heading downstairs to meet her stepfather.

Jon had set out plates and silverware on the table.

"Here," he said, motioning her over. His eyes traveled up her body and paused for a moment at her chest. "You look nice."

"Thanks." Jessa tried not to stare at the way his shirt fit his body, or the way his jeans hugged his muscular legs. He had always been a good looking guy, but the more she stared at him the more she felt that strange tension building in her again. She forced her eyes away. "Is there anything I can help you with?"

"Nope. Have a seat, everything's ready."

He placed a pot roast on the table, along with a plate full of green beans and another of mashed potatoes. It was like a little piece of home, a reminder of the family dinners she'd eaten when she was young, sitting across the table from her stepdad.

"Looks great, Jon," she said, helping herself to a slice of the meat. "You always were a great cook."

"Well eat up," Jon encouraged her. "You look so thin."

"I've been eating."

"Not enough. A growing girl needs her protein."

"I'm not a little kid anymore," Jessa said, but she helped herself to some more meat.

They ate in silence for a while, and Jessa savored the taste of a good meal. Even after being kicked out of her mother's house, her car still hadn't been fixed. She'd been living off ramen and peanut butter for the last two weeks. It was so nice to have a real home cooked meal again.

"So, Jess, tell me about what's going on with you. Last time we talked, you were saying you might transfer colleges?"

Jessa shrugged. "I don't know. I can't really afford it right now, anyway."

"Well, I'll always support you if you need money. You know that."

"I can't ask you for that, Dad. I'm not a kid anymore, and Mom was already pissed when I decided to go back to school. If I start asking people to pay my tuition..." She shook her head.

"Hey." Jon reached across the table and rested his hand on hers. "If there's ever anything you need, I'm here for you."

Jessa felt a surge of electricity at his touch, and she pulled her hand away. "I know, Dad. Thank you. I'll be fine."

"If you're not going to move to a new school, what are your plans?"

Jessa shrugged. "Get a job, save up enough money to move. Maybe transfer later."

"You don't have to work and go to school, Jessa. I can help you. Just until you're back on your feet."

"I couldn't."

"I can pay for your tuition, if you'll let me."

"It's not that. I just couldn't accept money from you. Not after Mom."

"Jess, I don't want to see you struggle. Especially not because of your mom. This has nothing to do with her. And besides," Jon paused for a moment as though he was thinking carefully about what he wanted to say next. "Maybe we could help each other."

"Help each other?"

"Yeah." Jon stood up and walked around the table. He rested his hand on Jessa's shoulder, and she looked up at him. "Come here. There's something I want to talk to you about."

He held out his hand, and Jessa took it, her heart pounding as she followed him into the living room.

"Why don't you sit down on the couch," he said.

"Okay."

She sat down, and he joined her. She felt her heart thumping in her chest. Jon was so close, and she couldn't help remembering the way his hands had traveled over her body in the shower. It had just been a fantasy, a weird dream brought on by the stress of the past few weeks. But now, here she was, sitting on the couch next to him, feeling that strange tension building between her thighs again.

"Jess," he said, turning toward her.

"Yeah, Dad?"

"I'm going to tell you something. It's not going to be easy for me to explain, but I want you to listen, okay?"

"Of course, Dad."

"This is about what I told you, that I'm going to help you, and you're going to help me. Jessa, I don't want to see you go through any trouble, but I'm not going to just give you the money you need."

"I don't mind working for it," she said.

"You want to work for Daddy?" Jon asked, his eyes drifting down Jessa's neck to the slight swells of her breasts.

"Like for your company?" Jessa squeaked.

"No," Jon laughed soflty. "Not for the business. I have a different sort of job for you."

"What do you mean?" Jessa was confused. She couldn't quite decipher the look on Jon's face, but there was a strange hunger in his eyes that she'd never seen before.

"Well," he said, "it's going to sound a little strange at first, but if you hear me out, I think we could both benefit."

"I don't understand," she said.

"What would you do if I told you I wanted to take care of you? But that I also needed you to take care of me."

"But how can I take care of you? I don' t have anything."

"You have your body, sweetheart."

"My body?"

Jon reached out and rested his hand on her thigh, his fingers caressing her. "I want you to give your body to me."

"Daddy, what are you talking about? What do you mean?"

"I mean," Jon said, "that I'm going to pay for your school, and all of your expenses, and even give you a little spending money. All I want is for you to let me use your body."

"What?"

"Have you ever been with a man before, Sweetheart?"

"No!"

"Would you like me to be your first?"

"I..." Jessa stuttered.

"You know, sweetheart, I'd make sure you were safe. You're a beautiful young girl, and I don't want to see anyone hurt you. You're so delicate. You need a real man to take care of you. Someone who can protect you, and help you, and take away all your pain."

"Daddy..." Jessa could barely breathe. "I..."

"Shh, shh. Don't answer. Just let me show you. Let Daddy take care of his little girl."

Before she knew what was happening, Jon leaned forward and kissed her.

Jessa felt like the breath had been sucked out of her. For a moment, she couldn't move, couldn't breathe. It was as though all her body's energy was centered in her mouth, on the lips where Jon's mouth met hers. She closed her eyes and savored the sensation, the way his hands traveled over her body, gently caressing her thighs, cupping her breasts. She didn't even realize how fast her heart was beating until she felt Jon's hand on her chest, his fingertips brushing the tops of her breasts.

He broke off the kiss, and Jessa gasped.

"Dad, what are you doing?"

"Just relax," he murmured. "Let Daddy make you feel good."

"Oh, god." Jessa felt light-headed. Her entire body was flushed, her nipples hard under the fabric of her dress. Jon's hand was on her chest, sliding over her breasts, squeezing them gently. His other hand moved to her legs, and his fingers brushed over the inside of her thighs, inching their way up toward her panties.

She couldn't think straight. The heat between her legs was intense, a hot wetness that spread through her body, making her shiver. She didn't know what was going on. All she knew was that her stepfather was kissing her, and his hands were all over her, and it was wrong, so wrong. But she couldn't bring herself to stop him.

She closed her eyes, letting the sensations wash over her. Her heart was pounding, and she felt as though her whole body was vibrating. She could feel the wetness spreading between her legs, soaking through her underwear.

Jon's hand slid up her thigh and under her dress, and she moaned softly. His fingers traced over her panties, gently stroking the wetness that had soaked through. He chuckled.

"See, Sweetheart? Look how wet you are for Daddy. You're such a good girl. My beautiful little girl."

He pulled the hem of her dress up over her stomach, and his hand slid under the waistband of her panties, his fingers caressing her pussy.

"Do you want Daddy to make you feel good?"

"Y-yes," she gasped.

"What was that?"

"Yes, Daddy."

"Say it again, sweetheart."

"Yes, Daddy, please."

"Good girl."

His fingers slipped inside her, and Jessa moaned. It was unlike anything she'd ever felt before. He worked them inside her slowly, teasing her, stretching her open. His thumb brushed against her clit, and she gasped.

"That's my good girl. Daddy's going to make you feel so good."

Jessa could barely breathe. Her body was on fire, and she could feel her heart racing. His fingers moved inside her, and she couldn't help but cry out.

"Oh, Daddy, yes!"

Jon pulled his fingers out and slid them up over her stomach and up her chest, pushing her dress up to expose her bra. He reached around her and unclasped it, pulling the fabric away from her body and letting her breasts fall free. His eyes lingered on her naked body, and she shivered.

"Look at those beautiful tits. You're so gorgeous, sweetheart."

"D-Daddy, I..."

"Shh. Let Daddy make you feel good."

"Ah...oh, Daddy, that feels so good..."

He was kissing her, his mouth traveling down her neck, his hands moving over her body. She could feel his erection pressing against her leg.

"God, Daddy, please..."

"Please what, baby?"

"I...I don't know. Just, please..."

"Don't worry. I'm going to make you feel so good."

He lifted her into his arms and carried her down the hall to his bedroom.

Jessa couldn't believe what was happening. It was all too much. His hands, his mouth. It was everything she had been dreaming about. She could barely breathe. He set her down on the bed, and he kissed her, his tongue exploring her mouth.

She was soaking wet, and she could feel her juices running down her thighs. She was so aroused, and she wanted him so badly. He reached down and stroked her pussy through her panties, and she gasped.

"Oh, Daddy, yes, please, more..."

"Don't worry, sweetheart. Daddy's going to give you everything you need."

He pulled her panties off and tossed them aside. He took her hand and pressed it against his erection. She could feel the size of him through his pants, and she shuddered.

"Daddy, it's so big."

"Don't worry, baby. It's going to feel so good."

He stripped down and tossed his clothes aside. His body was a work of art, chiseled muscles and taut skin. Jessa couldn't take her eyes off him. He was so big and strong, and his cock was so thick. She'd never imagined a man could be so big.

He got on the bed and positioned himself between her legs.

"You ready, sweetheart?"

"Yes, Daddy, please, I need it."

"It's going to hurt a little bit at first, but I need you to be a brave girl for Daddy. Can you do that?"

"Yes, Daddy."

He pushed his cock against her entrance, and she gasped. He was so big, and she was so small. She felt him push inside her, and she cried out.

"Daddy, it's too big!"

"Shh, shh, sweetheart. It's okay. Just relax. Let Daddy take care of you."

"Ah...oh, god, Daddy..."

He pushed further into her, and she cried out again. He was so big, and she felt like he was stretching her apart. But at the same time, it was the most incredible feeling she'd ever experienced. She'd never been so full, and it felt so good.

"That's a good girl," he whispered, and began to move inside her, slowly, gently. "See? Doesn't that feel good?"

"Yes, Daddy," she gasped. "It feels so good."

"You're such a good girl," he murmured. "Daddy's going to make you feel so good."

"Oh, god, Daddy, yes."

He began to thrust harder, and she moaned, her nails digging into his back. It was the most incredible feeling, and she could feel her body tightening around him.

"You like that, sweetheart? Does that feel good?"

"Yes, Daddy, oh god, yes!"

"I want you to come for Daddy," he said. "Come for me, baby."

She was lost in a haze of pleasure, and she couldn't think straight. She was so close, and she could feel her body shuddering. She was so close, and then...

"Oh, god, Daddy, yes!" she cried out as she came, her orgasm washing over her. She couldn't believe it, and she cried out as he continued to thrust into her, and the waves of pleasure crashed over her.

He kept going, his pace increasing, and she could feel his cock swelling inside her. She was so tight, and he was so big, and she wanted him so badly. She was so close again, and she could feel her body trembling.

"One more for Daddy," Jon groaned. "Be a good girl and give Daddy one more."

"Daddy, I...ah, fuck, Daddy, yes!"

She was so close, and he was thrusting into her, and she could feel her body shaking.

"Oh, god, Daddy, yes! Fuck, fuck, oh, god, Daddy, I'm coming, oh, god, yes!"

She was gasping and crying out, and he was thrusting into her, and he was so big, and she was coming again, and it was so good. It was like nothing she'd ever felt before, and it was the most amazing thing in the world.

"Fuck, sweetheart, open your mouth for Daddy," he growled.

He pulled his cock out and Jessa opened her mouth as wide as she could for him, tasting her own juices on him. He grabbed the back of her head and forced her down his length, and she gagged as he hit the back of her throat. She was trying not to choke, but the pleasure was so intense, and she wanted to please him so badly.

"Be a good girl and take it."

He was thrusting into her mouth, and she was sucking him, and he was moaning, and she was choking, and then he was coming, his cum shooting down her throat.

She was gulping it down, and he was holding her head in place, and it was the most intense thing she'd ever felt. It was like nothing else in the world.

He pulled out, and she was gasping for air, cum dripping down her chin, and he was kissing her, and she was kissing him back, and it was the most amazing feeling.

"Did you like that, sweetheart?"

"Y-yes, Daddy," she said.

"You were such a good girl. Daddy's going to give you everything you need."

"Thank you, Daddy."

"Now, get some rest. You've had a long day."

"Okay, Daddy."

He laid down next to her, and she curled up next to him, resting her head on his chest.

"Sleep tight, sweetheart."

"Night, Daddy."

"I love you."

"I love you too, Daddy."

They lay together, their bodies entwined, and Jessa fell asleep in the arms of her stepfather.

GET A FREE BOOK!

* * *

Be the first to find out about all of Lee Riley's new releases, book sales, and freebies by joining her VIP Mailing List. Join today and get a FREE book -- instantly!

Check Lee Riley's website spicybestsellers.com for more books.

* * *

ABOUT THE AUTHOR

* * *

Lee Riley is an adventurous writer who creates spicy short stories that challenge conventions and leave readers on the edge of their seats. Drawing inspiration from their travels, Lee explores the world with insatiable curiosity, using these experiences to craft stories that captivate readers.

When not writing, Lee indulges their passion for the outdoors, discovering new culinary delights, and making connections with people from all walks of life. Their love for adventure and zest for life is reflected in their work, which is daring, unconventional, and full of surprises.

More on www.spicybestsellers.com

* * *

LEE RILEY
Daddy's Naughty Girls 2
DEVOURED
BY HER STEPFATHER

LEE RILEY
Daddy's Naughty Girls 3
UNDRESSED
BY HER STEPFATHER

LEE RILEY
6 Parts!
One Price!
BETHANY'S
SUBMISSION
DOMESTIC DISCIPLINE
SPANKING ROMANCE

6 Books!
One Price!
BACK ALLEY
DISCIPLINE
DOMESTIC DISCIPLINE
BUNDLE

LEE RILEY
5 Books! One Price!
BACK DOOR DISCIPLINE
DOMESTIC DISCIPLINE BUNDLE

LEE RILEY
6 Books! One Price!
GET PUNISHED
DOMESTIC DISCIPLINE BUNDLE

LEE RILEY
6 Books!
One Price!
GET SPANKED
DOMESTIC DISCIPLINE
BUNDLE

* * *